TOWER HAMLETS

91 000 006 621 24 7

KT-407-250

SPACE ACE

ERIC BROWN & TONY ROSS

SPACE ACE

Barrington Stoke

To James, Lou, Monty and Theo Lovegrove

First published in 2017 in Great Britain by
Barrington Stoke Ltd
18 Walker Street, Edinburgh, EH3 7LP

www.barringtonstoke.co.uk

Reprinted 2018, 2019

This 4u2read edition based on *Space Ace*
(Barrington Stoke, 2005)

Text © 2017 Eric Brown
Illustrations © 2005 Tony Ross

The moral right of Eric Brown and Tony Ross to be identified
as the author and illustrator of this work has been asserted in
accordance with the Copyright, Designs and Patents Act, 1988

All rights reserved. No part of this publication may be
reproduced in whole or in any part in any form without the
written permission of the publisher

A CIP catalogue record for this book is available
from the British Library upon request

ISBN: 978-1-78112-725-4

Printed in Great Britain by Charlesworth Press

CONTENTS

Chapter 1
Blast-Off

The wall-screen in my room came on. It was Grandad.

"I've done it, Billy!" he said.

I jumped up. "You have? You've really done it?"

Grandad grinned. He looked happy, with his wild grey hair like a mad professor and his big smile.

"I've got the *Falcon Mark II* spaceship running," he said. "I was thinking ..." He stopped and looked at me.

"Yes?" I asked. My heart was beating like a drum.

"I was thinking, Billy, that you might like to test fly it with me?"

I was so excited that I couldn't speak. I just nodded.

"Good," Grandad said. "Meet me at the yard in five minutes."

I ran out of my room and grabbed my jacket. Mum was in the hall.

"Billy," Mum said, "where are you off to?"

"Grandad's," I said.

"You're not to go in any of his old spaceships!" she said.

"Don't you trust him?" I asked.

"It's not that I don't trust him," she said. "It's just that when he was an astronaut, he had a crash in space. Perhaps you should ask him about it. And remember – no spaceships, OK?"

But I was already running out of the house.

Grandad had been an astronaut for many years. He was the first person to set foot on Mars, back in 2035. That was 40 years ago, and now Grandad was too old to be an astronaut.

Now Grandad ran a spaceship junk yard instead. It was full of fins and wings and huge engines. There were whole spaceships in the yard too. I loved to climb inside, strap myself into the pilot seat and pretend I was off to space. It was amazing to think that all this scrap metal had once travelled to other planets and far away stars.

Grandad liked to build new spaceships from all the bits in the junk yard. He also kept a big journal full of amazing facts about the solar system. I was always reading it! I thought about what Mum had told me. Grandad had never said anything about a crash. Was that why he had stopped being an astronaut?

Grandad's head poked out of a silver spaceship shaped like the head of an arrow.

"Welcome aboard the *Falcon*!" he said.

I ran up the ramp and into the ship.

"It's fantastic!" I said. There were two seats in front of a large screen. There were more seats behind, like in a bus, with screens all round the side.

"It used to be a tourist ship," Grandad told me. "In the old days it took people around the Solar System, to see all the planets."

"Can we do that?" I cried.

"No," Grandad said. "We'll just make a quick orbit of the Earth, to make sure the ship works. Strap yourself in the co-pilot's seat and we'll blast off."

I jumped into the seat and strapped myself in.

I wondered if I should ask Grandad about the crash, but I decided to leave it till later.

Grandad sat in the pilot's seat and ran his hands over the control panel.

"Hold tight, Billy!" he yelled. "We're taking off!"

The *Falcon* roared and shot into the air like a bullet.

Chapter 2
Mercury

I looked at a screen and saw the city get smaller and smaller. We had to go fast to escape the Earth's gravity, which tried to pull us back.

"We're leaving Planet Earth behind us, Billy," Grandad said. "Soon we'll be in space. My word, this does bring back memories!"

Soon Earth was a small ball below us. Grandad tapped the control panel with a frown.

"What's wrong?" I asked.

"The controls aren't working," he said. "We're heading *away* from Earth."

"EMERGENCY! EMERGENCY!" a loud voice cried.

"What was that?" I said.

"The ship's computer," Grandad said. "Something's gone wrong."

I gripped the arms of my seat and stared at the screen. All I could see was black space – and then, far away from us, the sun.

"We're heading for the *sun!*" I whispered.

Grandad was pressing button after button, but nothing happened. Sweat ran down his face.

"EMERGENCY! EMERGENCY!" the computer cried.

Grandad said, "Computer, why aren't the controls working?"

The computer said, "OVERRIDE! OVERRIDE!"

"What does that mean?" I asked.

"It means that the computer that was in the tour ship has taken over," Grandad said.

Just then I heard a sound behind me.
"Welcome to Solar System Tours!" a voice said.
"We hope you enjoy your trip around the Solar
System!"

A man in a blue uniform was standing
behind us. He was talking to the empty seats
around him. He looked like a ghost – I could see
right through him!

"It's a tour guide hologram!" Grandad said.
"A kind of image made from light."

"But we're still heading towards the sun!" I cried.

"Wrong, Space Ace," the guide said.

"My name's Billy!" I said.

"We're heading towards Mercury," the guide said.

"Billy, it looks like you got what you wanted," Grandad said. "We're going on a tour of the Solar System!"

"You're right, sir!" the guide said. "I'll take you on a tour of all the planets in Sol's System. Sol is the name of our sun, by the way. If you have any questions, please ask!"

"Great!" I said.

"To our right," the guide said, "you can see Mercury. It is the smallest planet in our Solar System. Its atmosphere gets blown away by

solar winds – so it has no air or gases around it. It is the closest planet to the sun – only 58 million kilometres away."

I stared out at the tiny grey planet, covered with thousands of round crater holes.

"Mercury," our guide said, "moves around the sun very fast and so it has the shortest year of any planet. Just 88 Earth days long! During the night, it's very cold – 170°C below zero. But during the day it's hot – around 430°C. It would be impossible for human life to exist on Mercury."

I watched as we looped around the planet and flew away.

"And now we are heading towards the second planet out from the sun," our guide said. "Venus."

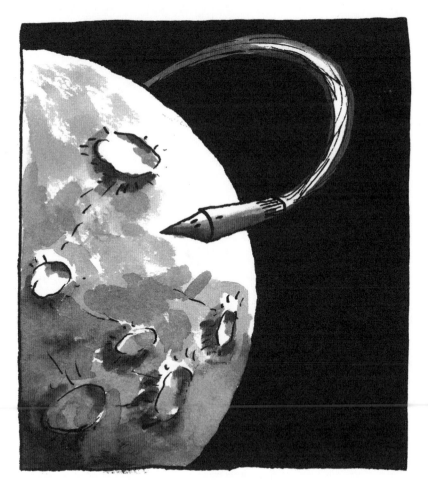

Chapter 3
Venus

"How long will we be in space?" Grandad asked the guide.

"Just two days," the guide said. "Top speed all the way!"

The guide stepped forward and pointed at a screen. "In front of us now you can see the planet Venus, which is 108 million kilometres from the sun."

The planet filled the screen. It was covered with what looked like pale yellow clouds.

"Venus is the closest planet to Earth," the guide said. "But it is even hotter than Mercury. Clouds made from carbon dioxide trap heat on the surface and don't let it escape. The surface temperature is 480°C. That is more than four times hotter than boiling water! In 1975, an unmanned space probe landed on Venus and sent back pictures for almost an hour before it burned up. These pictures showed a surface of sharp rocks and huge stones."

We sped away from Venus and I watched the planet get smaller and smaller on the screen.

"Soon we will pass Planet Earth," the guide said, "but I think you know all about this planet already! After Earth, we will fly close to Mars."

'Mars ...' I thought. I looked at Grandad and wondered if he was thinking about the planet he had visited more than 40 years ago.

Chapter 4

Mars

We passed Earth, a round ball covered with blue seas and bright white cloud.

"I'll try and get in touch with your mum," Grandad said. "She'll want to know where you've got to."

"No, don't!" I said. "You see ... Mum didn't want me to go into space with you. She said something about a crash."

Grandad put an arm round me. "Billy," he said, "I've never told you before. I *was* in a crash. It was my fault ..."

His eyes had a faraway look.

"We were on our way back from Saturn," he told me. "We were in the asteroid belt and ... Well, I crashed the ship into a spinning asteroid. I lost control. It was my fault ..." He stopped, then said, "One man died. I was hurt. That was the last trip I ever did. The truth was, the Space Agency didn't want me, after the crash."

He turned away and stared at the screen. I didn't know what to say. I just reached out and held his hand.

An hour later I looked at my screen and saw the Red Planet – Mars.

The guide said, "In the year 2035, Commander William Jones was the first person to set foot on Mars."

I looked at Grandad. I could see tears in his eyes as he stared down at the red planet.

"Mars is –" the guide began.

"Please," Grandad said, "I'll tell Billy about Mars, if you don't mind."

The guide fell silent.

Grandad said, "Mars is the second smallest planet in the solar system, and is 228 million kilometres from the sun. It's very cold on the surface. When my team and I were there, the temperature could be anything between minus 27°C and minus 133°C. You would freeze to death if you didn't wear a space-suit to protect you."

He smiled and shook his head. "Some scientists thought that life might exist on Mars. We looked everywhere, but we didn't find anything. Many millions of years ago, there might have been life. But Mars has been slowly moving away from the sun, getting a little colder all the time."

I stared down at the craters, and the long lines scored across the face of the planet, which looked like canals.

"We landed near Olympus Mons," Grandad said. "It's a huge, dead volcano – 26 kilometres high. There, you can see it!"

He pointed, and I saw a big circle, dark red against the pinkish sands of Mars.

"And there," Grandad said, "are the two moons of Mars, Phobos and Deimos."

I watched them spin past the ship. They looked like knobbly potatoes.

"Phobos is 27 kilometres long," Grandad said. "Deimos is smaller, just 15 kilometres at its longest point. They're getting closer to Mars, and one day they'll crash into its surface."

The ship turned, and headed away from the red planet. Grandad reached out and gripped my hand.

"In a short while," the guide said, "get ready for the fantastic sight of Jupiter!"

Chapter 5
Jupiter

"That's amazing!" I cried out, three hours later.

"Jupiter!" the guide said. "It's about 778 million kilometres from the sun, and it's by far the biggest planet in the Solar System."

Not only was it the biggest – it was also the most colourful. It was covered with stripes of cloud – orange and brown and yellow.

"Jupiter is what we call a gas giant," the guide said. "You cannot see the surface of the planet. It has a rocky core about the size of Earth, but this is covered by a layer of liquid metallic hydrogen 33,000 kilometres thick. On top of this is a covering of liquid non-metallic hydrogen 22,000 kilometres thick, and then a thin atmosphere of hydrogen and helium gas, just 1,000 kilometres thick."

"There's the red spot!" I said. I was very
excited.

Jupiter was famous for its Great Red Spot.

"The red spot is really a storm," the
guide told us. "It has been raging round
Jupiter for hundreds of years. The spot is

40,000 kilometres long and 11,000 kilometres wide. So wide that Earth could fit into it three times."

We flew closer to Jupiter, and it filled the entire screen.

"This is as close as we can come to the planet," the guide said. "Jupiter throws out a lot of radiation, which is dangerous to humans."

"Look," Grandad said, "the moons."

We were flying next to two big moons, and I could see other moons in the distance, all circling around giant Jupiter.

"Jupiter has at least 67 moons," the guide said. "One of them, Ganymede, is the biggest moon in the Solar System. It's even bigger than the planets of Mercury and Pluto. Scientists think that a long time ago, some of the moons might have been planets like Earth and Mars, but they were captured by Jupiter's strong magnetic field, and now they circle the planet for ever."

I looked at the guide. "Have we sent any unmanned rockets to Jupiter?"

"Yes – eight spacecraft have visited Jupiter so far. In the 1970s, *Pioneer 10* and *Pioneer 11* sent back the first close-up pictures of Jupiter and its moons. And in 2016, NASA's *Juno* sent the closest images ever seen of Jupiter."

On the screen I saw a faint ring system. I pointed. "I didn't know Jupiter had rings!" I said.

The guide grinned. "In 1979, the *Voyager 1* probe discovered a system of rings made up of millions of tiny grains of dust."

"Could we live on the moons?" I asked.

"Perhaps on the outer moons," the guide said. "But even then we would have to live in special domes to protect us from Jupiter's strong radiation."

I stared at the planet as we moved away. "Goodbye, Jupiter," I whispered. "Goodbye, Great Red Spot!"

Chapter 6
Saturn

"Saturn is the second biggest planet in the Solar System," the guide said. "And do you know why it is famous?"

"Because of its rings!" I said.

"Correct."

I thought that Saturn was the most lovely thing I had ever seen. Around the middle of the light brown planet was the famous ring system.

Each ring was a different colour, silver and gold and black, all shining in the light of the planet.

"Saturn is another gas giant," the guide said. "Like Jupiter, it has a rocky core. And like Jupiter it has a layer of liquid metallic hydrogen but it's thinner, about 15,000 kilometres thick. Above this is another layer – this time of liquid non-metallic hydrogen which is 25,000 kilometres thick. On top of all this is a thin atmosphere of hydrogen and helium gases."

The guide pointed at the screen. "Saturn has more moons than any other planet. Do you know how many moons it's got, Space Ace?"

"My name is Billy!" I said. "And I think it has about 150 moons and smaller moonlets that we know of."

"That's right!" he said. "Scientists think that perhaps it once had many more, but they smashed into each other and shattered into millions of bits of rock. These tiny bits of rock formed into the rings we can see today."

"How far away is Saturn from the sun?" I asked.

The guide smiled. "It is 1.4 billion kilometres away."

'1.4 billion kilometres!' I thought. I looked at the rear screen. Our sun was a tiny shining star in the distance.

Grandad was staring out at Saturn. "My very last mission was to Saturn," he said. He looked sad.

I didn't ask him about it.

Chapter 7
Uranus

It was another three hours before we reached the next planet – Uranus.

We were now even further away from home.

The guide said, "Uranus is 2.9 billion kilometres away from the sun. It is smaller than Saturn and has an atmosphere of hydrogen, helium and methane – no human could breathe on it! Uranus is a gas giant, like

Jupiter and Saturn, but it is an ice giant. Also, like Saturn, it has a ring system."

Uranus was not as lovely as Saturn. It was pale blue-green, and its rings were faint and tilted towards us.

I pointed. "Is that a moon?"

"Correct, Space Ace!"

I was getting mad by then. "My name," I said, "is not Space Ace! It's Billy!"

From the corner of my eye I saw Grandad laughing. "When we're back on Earth, I'll fix the computer program," he said.

The guide was saying, "Uranus has more than 25 moons. The largest is Titania."

We raced past Uranus.

"And now for Neptune!"

Chapter 8
Neptune

"Now we are 4.5 billion kilometres away from the sun," the guide said, "and in front of us you can see the planet Neptune."

Every day I walked a kilometre to school – and Neptune was 4.5 *billion* kilometres from the sun. I felt dizzy thinking about it!

Neptune was the same size as Uranus, and it had 4 rings. It was a bright blue colour and hazy. It looked cold.

"Like Uranus," the guide said, "the atmosphere of Neptune is made up of hydrogen, helium and methane. The weather on Neptune is perhaps the oddest thing about the planet. Storms last for hundreds of years, and high-speed solar winds blow at over 600 kilometres per hour! Just try to hold onto your umbrella in that!"

"Does Neptune have any moons?" I asked.

"It has 13 or 14 moons that we know of," the guide said. "The biggest is Triton, and it is famous for being one of the coldest objects in the Solar System – its surface is 235°C below zero."

We flew around the planet, and minutes later the guide said, "If you look to your left, you will see Triton."

We raced past a great brown ball. We were so close that I thought for a second that we were going to hit it.

"There is another interesting fact about Triton," the guide said. "As far as we know, it is the only moon in the solar system that orbits in the opposite direction to the rotation of its planet."

I thought about that, and all the other facts the guide had told me. What a story I would write on Monday, when my teacher asked the class what we did at the weekend!

"Your tour of the Solar System is almost over," the guide said. "The last stop is Pluto."

Chapter 9
Pluto

We were out on the very edge of the Solar System now, nearly six billion kilometres from the sun.

"People used to think that Pluto was the ninth planet in our solar system, but now they call it a 'dwarf planet'," the guide said. "Dwarf planets may provide the best evidence about the origins of our solar system. Scientists think that once Pluto may have been a moon of Neptune, and that it smashed into another moon, which pushed it out to the very edge of the Solar System."

We were very close to Pluto. It was tiny and round and made of ice, like a bright blue snowball.

"Pluto's surface temperature is around 225°C below zero," the guide said. "It is made up of frozen methane, which is why it is blue. It takes more than 248 years to go round the sun."

We shot round Pluto in a huge loop.

"On the screen on your left, you will see Charon. This is Pluto's largest moon, and is about half the size of Pluto."

We raced away from Pluto and its moon and off towards the sun, which was a tiny twinkling star in the distance.

"And now we begin the long flight home," the guide said. "We will reach Earth in just under one day. But there is one more thing to see before then."

"The asteroids!" I said.

Chapter 10
Asteroids, and Home

"Let's get some sleep," Grandad said. "The guide will wake us when we reach the asteroid belt."

We pulled two bunk beds from the wall and lay down. But my head was too full of all the fantastic sights I'd seen to sleep.

I must have fallen asleep at last, because the computer woke me, calling, "EMERGENCY! EMERGENCY!"

"What's happening?" Grandad asked.

We ran to our seats and strapped ourselves in.

I stared at the screen and gasped.

We were in the middle of the asteroid belt!

The guide said, "The asteroid belt lies
between Mars and Jupiter."

"Please, guide," Grandad said, "shut up!"

The guide took no notice.

"Asteroids can be as small as a house or as big as a few hundred kilometres across," he said. "They are made of rock and metal."

The ship was flying itself past the asteroids, which tumbled past like a torrent of falling stones. I thought we were going to crash into one at any second.

I looked at Grandad. He was staring with wide eyes at the screen. I wondered if he was remembering the crash, all those years ago.

"There are more than 50,000 asteroids in the belt," the guide went on.

I really didn't want to know that! It seemed that every one of them was trying to smash into us.

At that second, we did hit something. The ship shook and clanged like a bell.

"EMERGENCY! AUTOPILOT DAMAGED. THE PILOT MUST TAKE OVER AND FLY ON MANUAL!"

Grandad looked over at me. "That means I've got to get us through the asteroid belt myself, without the help of the computer."

I held onto my seat while Grandad tapped at the control panel. His hands moved in a blur, as he plotted our course past the tumbling asteroids.

I covered my eyes when a big rock loomed up at us – but the smash never came.

I opened my eyes. We were still in the asteroid belt. Big rocks rushed towards us, but Grandad steered the ship out of the way again and again.

I held onto my seat as we swerved this way and that. It was like being on the fastest rollercoaster in the world.

"Hold on tight, Billy!" Grandad yelled.

I gripped the arms of my seat and shouted in fear. A huge rock filled the screen, but at the very last second Grandad pulled the ship up and away.

"Done it!" he said.

Seconds later he was steering us past the last of the asteroids, and he was smiling like I'd never seen him smile before.

Minutes later Grandad sat back in his seat. "I've done it, Billy," he said. "I've done it. We're safe."

Clear space lay ahead of us, and in the distance I saw the small, blue shape of Planet Earth.

I flung myself at Grandad and hugged him.

Two hours later we landed back in the junk yard, between the piles of scrap metal and old starships.

We sat in silence for a while, and then I said, "Grandad, that was the best weekend I've ever had in all my life!"

He smiled and shook his head. "I never thought I'd get us past the asteroids ..."

"Perhaps," I said, "we could go back one day and this time land on Mars."

"That would be great," Grandad said. "But first I've got to get you back home in time for Sunday dinner."

As we left the junk yard, I looked up into the night sky.

"Grandad," I said, "the guide never told us about *our* moon!"

Grandad laughed. "Then I will," he said.

As we walked home hand in hand, Grandad told me about the moon.

"The moon is Earth's only satellite," he said, "and it is 384,000 kilometres away from Earth. It has no air and no life – but it helps make Earth a more liveable planet for us. In 1969 Neil Armstrong became the first person to walk on the moon. He was another Space Ace!"

SIZZLING FACTS about the Sun!

1. The sun is 4.5 billion years old and almost 150 million kilometres from Earth

2. The temperature at the core of the sun is 15 million Kelvin

3. In a few billion years' time, the sun will swell into a huge red ball so big that it will engulf the Earth. It will be 150 times bigger than it is now, and shine a thousand times brighter

Miraculous facts about Mercury!

1. Mercury is the smallest planet in the Solar System, and it is the closest planet to the sun

2. Mercury is named after the Roman messenger god

3. Mercury has no moons

Feed Graham the Martian Gerbil before the next space flight GD

Fantastic facts about Venus!

1. A year on Venus – the time it takes the planet to move around the sun – lasts for about 225 Earth days

2. Venus is yellow because of sulphuric acid in its atmosphere. This may come from active volcanoes on the surface

3. Venus has no moons

4. Venus is named after the Greek goddess of love and beauty

Forty years ago Today I walked on Mars

GD

Marvellous Facts about Mars!

1. Mars takes 687 Earth days to move around the sun – so a year on Mars is nearly twice as long as an Earth year!

2. Mars is named after the Roman god of war

3. The atmosphere on Mars is made up of lots of different gases, carbon dioxide, nitrogen, argon, and tiny amounts of oxygen, carbon monoxide and water vapour. It is thin and deadly to human beings!

Jubilant facts about Jupiter!

1. Jupiter moves slowly around the sun, so that a year lasts for 12 Earth years

2. Jupiter spins very fast, so that a day lasts for almost ten Earth hours

3. The cloud-top temperature is minus 150°C

4. Jupiter is named after the ruler of the Roman gods

Fabulous Facts about Saturn!

1. A year on Saturn lasts for almost 30 Earth years

2. A day on Saturn – the time it takes Saturn to spin on its axis – lasts for ten Earth hours

3. The cloud-top temperature is minus 180°C

4. Saturn is named after the Roman god of farming and the harvest

Remember Billy's birthday present – he likes Luna Chocs!
G.D.

Ultimate facts about Uranus!

1. Uranus is named after the Greek god of the sky

2. Uranus was discovered in 1781 by William Herschel

3. The cloud-top temperature is minus 220°C

4. Uranus is four times larger than Earth, and it is the third largest planet in the Solar System

Nifty facts about Neptune!

1. Neptune is named after the Roman god of the sea

2. John Couch Adams, Urbain Le Verrier and Johann Gottfried Galle discovered Neptune in the 1840s

3. A day on Neptune lasts for just over 19 Earth hours

4. Neptune is the fourth largest planet in the Solar System

Tomorrow.
meet Space Joe
at the Pluto
Pub for a
pint of
Jupitor Juice!
G.D.

Four Facts about **Pluto!**

1. Pluto spins slowly on its axis, so that a day on Pluto lasts for six Earth days and it takes almost 250 years to orbit the sun

2. Its atmosphere is made up of nitrogen, methane and carbon monoxide.

3. Pluto was discovered by Clyde Tombaugh in 1930

Buy a pair of space socks! You can wear them all week and they won't smell! *G.D.*

4. Pluto is named after the Roman god of the underworld

Famous People in Space!

1. The Russian Yuri Gagarin was the first person to go into space when he orbited the Earth in 1961

2. In 1962 John H. Glenn was the first American to fly around the Earth

3. In 1963 the Russian Valentina Tereshkova became the first woman in space

4. In 1965 the Russian Alexei Leonov was the first person to walk in space

Our books are tested
for children and young people by
children and young people.

Thanks to everyone who consulted on
a manuscript for their time and effort in
helping us to make our books better
for our readers.